PETS

D0581244

MONKEY MADNESS

Jan Burchett and Sara Vogler

Illustrated by Alex Paterson

Orion
Children's Books

First published in Great Britain in 2014
by Orion Children's Books
a division of the Orion Publishing Group Ltd
Orion House
5 Upper St Martin's Lane
London WC2H 9EA
An Hachette UK company

3 5 7 9 10 8 6 4 2

A catalogue record for this book is available from the British Library.

ISBN 978 1 4440 1184 5

Printed in Great Britain by Clays Ltd, St Ives plc

www.orionbooks.co.uk

For Olive Grace Heywood,
with love from Great Auntie Sara
S.V.

For Kieran
A.P.

CONTENTS

Wonky Trolley

Tom and his friend Daisy were in Tom's garden. They were going to help Tom's dog, Fizz, investigate ants.

"Hurry up," called Fizz as he raced up to the flowerbeds. He wiggled his trumpet nose. "I need to start investigating."

Dogs can't usually speak.

And dogs don't usually have trumpet noses and they're not usually purple with yellow spots.

Fizz was a very unusual dog.

In fact, he wasn't a dog at all.

He was just pretending to be a dog.

Fizz was really a Satnik from the planet Saturn.

And he wasn't the only one. There were other Satniks. They were pretending to be Earth pets as well. Their spaceship had splash-landed in Tom's pond. They were on a secret mission to investigate Earth.

"I hope I find an ant," said Fizz, poking among the bushes. "I want to see it hopping about. And I can't wait to have a ride in its pouch."

"That's not an ant," laughed Tom. "That's a kangaroo!"

"No, it's not," said Fizz. "It's an ant. I'll show you on my Satpad. It knows everything about Earth animals."

He twisted his ear.

Ping!

A silver cube shot out, transformed itself into a tiny computer and landed

on his hand. He tapped the keys and an
image shimmered in the air.

"That's a kangaroo," said Daisy.

"Are you sure?" asked Fizz.

"Positive," said Daisy. "Don't forget,
your Satpads are always getting their
animals in a muddle."

"Zoops!" said Fizz, giving it a shake.
"I expect the sprungles are still flobbered
from when our spaceship nearly hit Mars.
I must remember to fix them."

Their friend Zack came running down
the path. He was carrying a shopping bag
with big bright flowers on it.

"Zack's got a moving garden!" Fizz
exclaimed, sniffing the shopping bag in
excitement. "Perhaps there are ants inside."

"It's not a garden," said Zack. "It's
a shopping bag – to put things in when
you go shopping. This one belongs to
my gran."

"I thought it was a bit small for a garden," said Fizz. "Is shopping fun?"

"No," said Tom.

"Especially not at the supermarket," said Daisy. "Supermarkets are really big and it takes ages to find all the things you want to buy."

"I've got to go to the supermarket for Gran," groaned Zack. "She said I must take her special bag."

"What have you got to buy?" asked Daisy.

"Two buns and a toothbrush," said Zack.

"You don't need a bag for that," said Daisy.

"Most of all not a big flowery one," said Tom in disgust.

"Exactly," said Zack. "And it's heavy. So I'm going to leave it here and pick it up on the way back."

"No!" squeaked the bag. "I'm coming
to the supermarket too."

A blue furry creature jumped out.
It had big round eyes and two antennae.
It looked like a mop.

"I didn't know you were in there,
Zingle!" said Zack in surprise. "No wonder
the bag was so heavy!"

Zingle was a Satnik like Fizz. She lived
with Zack and everyone thought she
was a cat — a rare blue mop-haired cat.

"I heard you were going shopping so I hopped in," Zingle explained. "I want to investigate supermarkets. I want to see the pears."

"They're yummy," said Tom. "Mum got some yesterday and I ate them all."

"Silly Earthling!" squeaked Zingle. "You can't eat pears. They're big and furry with sharp claws and they growl. Look." She twiddled her antennae.

Ping!

Her Satpad flew out of her fur and landed on her paw.

An image shimmered in the air.

"They're not pears," laughed Daisy. "They're bears."

"They certainly don't sell bears at supermarkets," added Zack.

"Our Satpads are still getting their animal facts in a muddle," said Fizz.

"Zoops!" squeaked Zingle. "But I do want to investigate the supermarket."

"Me too," said Fizz. "Tom's mum always brings back lovely things from there, like Wheaty Krisps. They're my favourite Earth cereal."

"Supermarkets are boring," said Zack. "You'll wish you'd stayed at home."

"Your parents drag you round to look at soup and sausages and stuff," said Tom.

"That sounds interesting!" squeaked Zingle.

"And sometimes you get a trolley with a wonky wheel," said Daisy. "It never goes where you want it to."

"That sounds *very* interesting!" squeaked Zingle.

"We're definitely coming to investigate the supermarket, Zack," said Fizz. "Then I can buy some Wheaty Krisps."

"Great idea!" said Tom. "You'll have fun shopping with the Satniks, Zack."

"You can't come," Zack told Fizz and Zingle. "You might be seen."

"You know adults would get very silly if they knew you were aliens," Daisy reminded them.

"No one will know," said Fizz. "Don't forget, we look like an ordinary dog and cat."

"But dogs and cats aren't allowed in supermarkets," said Zack.

"I've got an idea," said Daisy. "We'll all go. We'll disguise Fizz and Zingle as babies.

Then they can sit in the trolley. They're just the right size for the baby seats."

"Cosmic!" said Tom. "I'll get some hats and scarves for them. No one will guess they're aliens then."

"Can we have a wonky trolley?" asked Fizz as Tom plonked a bobble hat over Zingle's antennae.

"If we have to," said Daisy.

"We'd better take Gran's shopping bag after all," said Zack. "You two can hide in it till we get there."

As they arrived at the supermarket, it started to rain.

Zingle began to roll about the shopping bag, squeaking at the top of her voice. "I don't want to get wet."

"Zingle doesn't like getting wet," said Fizz, scrambling out of the way.

"We know," said Tom. "Don't worry, Zingle. We'll go inside. It doesn't rain in supermarkets!"

Daisy found a trolley with wonky wheels. Fizz and Zingle hopped into the baby seats.

When Daisy pushed the trolley forwards, it bumped along sideways.

When she pushed it sideways, it skidded backwards.

"Are you sure you want this trolley?" panted Daisy.

"Positive," said Fizz.

"It's nice and wonky," squeaked Zingle.

A girl went by with an umbrella.

"She's got her own roof!" Zingle looked amazed.

"That's an umbrella," Zack told her.

"Silly Earthling," squeaked Zingle. "It's a roof – and it's just what I need to keep me dry. I'll buy one in the supermarket."

At last Tom, Zack and Daisy managed to heave the trolley into the supermarket.

"I've made a shopping list," said Fizz,
"so we don't forget anything."

Ping!

His Satpad flew out of his ear. He
tapped a key and a list shimmered in the
air in front of them.

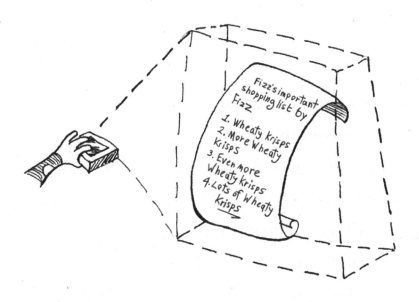

"Make me a shopping list!" demanded
Zingle.

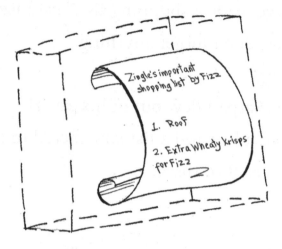

Fizz tapped the keys again. Another list shimmered in the air.

"Fizz is good at lists," squeaked Zingle happily.

An old woman walked past. She stopped and stared at the Satniks.

"Don't go too near our babies," warned Zack.

"They're very young," said Daisy.

"You might give them germs," added Tom.

But the old woman bent down and peered at them. She jumped back in surprise. "What ugly twins!" she exclaimed.

"Silly Earthling," squeaked Zingle loudly. "We're not twins!"

Lots of shoppers stopped and stared.

Tom, Zack and Daisy looked at each other in horror.

But, to their surprise, the old woman was smiling. She tickled Zingle on the top of her hat. "What a clever baby," she cooed. "You look too small to be able to talk."

"I'm not a baby!" squeaked Zingle.

"Sorry," said Tom, "we're in a hurry."

They dragged the trolley away.

"That was close," said Zack. "Now you Satniks must stay where you are."

"Of course we will," said Fizz.

"And don't speak to any more humans," said Daisy.

"Except us, of course," said Tom.

"Of course we won't," squeaked Zingle.

Tom, Zack and Daisy began to push the trolley towards the toothbrush aisle.

"Wheaty Krisps first!" announced Fizz. "I'll use my super Satpower. It'll find them before you can say jumping jimperflidgets!"

Ping!

His Satpad flew out of his ear. He tapped the keys.

Bleep . . . bleep . . . bleep went the Satpad.

"Follow me!" Fizz announced. He jumped out of his clothes, hopped onto a shelf and disappeared round a corner.

"We have to catch him," said Daisy, "before someone else does!"

"That would be a disaster," said Zack.

They heaved the trolley round the corner to the breakfast cereals.

"There's no sign of Fizz," said Zack.

Bleep . . . bleep . . . bleep!

"That'll be his Satpad," said Tom.

"Follow that bleep!" cried Zack.

They hurtled into the cheese aisle.

"We're coming, Fizz!" squeaked Zingle.

But the bleeping wasn't Fizz. It was the old woman. She was holding a mobile phone and it was bleeping loudly. She was so surprised to see the trolley rattling towards her that she dropped her shopping basket.

"Sorry," said Daisy, picking up the old woman's pineapple. "We've got a wonky trolley."

"And now I've got a wonky pineapple!" said the old woman. She walked off, tutting.

Bleep . . . bleep . . . bleep!

"Follow that bleep!" said Tom.

They dashed towards a tall tower of toilet rolls.

But the trolley wouldn't stop.

Kerflumph! It crashed into the tower. The toilet rolls fell in a heap.

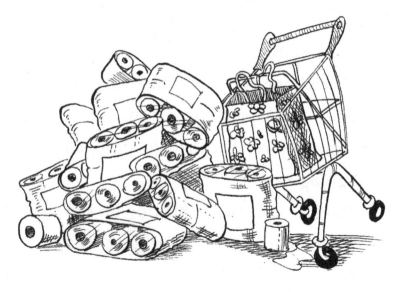

"Zoops!" squeaked Zingle. "That was fun."

Bleep! went the heap of toilet rolls.

"Fizz is under there," cried Daisy.

The three friends dug frantically.

But they didn't find Fizz.

Instead they uncovered a shop assistant with a price-checking machine.

Bleep! went the price-checking machine.

"Sorry," said Tom as they helped to build the tower of toilet rolls again. "We've got a wonky trolley."

"And now I've got a wonky price-checking machine," said the shop assistant. She walked off, shaking it crossly.

"Where can Fizz be?" said Daisy.

"And where's Zingle?" gasped Zack, pointing at Zingle's empty hat and scarf.

Zingle had gone!

"We'd better split up and look for them," said Tom.

"We can't!" said Zack. "It needs all three of us to make the trolley go."

"Agreed," said Daisy. "Let's find Zingle first."

"I bet she's looking for a roof!" exclaimed Zack.

They pushed the trolley along to the umbrellas. The umbrellas were scattered all over the floor.

"Zingle's definitely been here," said Daisy.

An assistant marched up.

"Did you do this?" she asked sternly.

"No," said Tom. "It was . . ."

". . . our trolley," Zack put in quickly.

"That's right," said Tom.

"It's a wonky trolley," explained Daisy.

"Well, make sure you clear everything up," said the assistant. She walked off, giving them a suspicious glare.

At last the umbrellas were back in place.

"Help! Get me down!" came a squeaky
voice. It was coming from a tin of beans.

Tom had never heard a tin of beans talk
before. Apart from the time in the kitchen
when one fell out of the cupboard and
hurt itself.

"That's Zingle," said Zack.

A shop assistant was putting Zingle
onto a shelf next to the dusters.

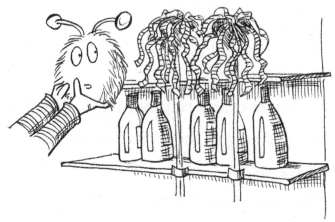

"This mop can talk!"
the assistant exclaimed.

"I'm not a mop," squeaked Zingle.
She began to roll up and down, squeaking
crossly.

"It's a talking mop," said Zack quickly.

"It talks to you while it does the
housework," explained Tom.

27

"I promised my dad I'd get him one," said Daisy.

She grabbed Zingle and put her in the bottom of the trolley.

"That's better!" Zingle had a big smile on her face.

"They're called Happy Mops," said Tom.

They dragged the trolley away backwards.

"Where's Fizz?" squeaked Zingle.

"We're still looking for him," Daisy told her.

"And we must look for a roof too," squeaked Zingle. "I tried some but they were too big."

They came to the gardening section. It was full of people buying seeds and watering cans.

"There's a roof!" Zingle jumped up and down in the trolley. "On that funny little man with the red cheeks and the pointy hat."

A garden gnome was sitting in a wheelbarrow. He was holding a bright yellow umbrella.

"It's a perfect roof," squeaked Zingle. "You can buy it for me."

"Then we'll have to buy the gnome too," said Daisy.

"No problem," said Zack. "Gran will love it. I'll tell her it's a toothbrush holder – for her new toothbrush."

Zack put the gnome in the trolley next to Zingle.

"Now to find Fizz," said Zack.

"I can see him," Zingle was looking down the aisle. "There's his nose."

"That's not his nose," said Tom. "It's a Hoover hose."

"A Hoover like Zack has in his house?" squeaked Zingle eagerly. "I want to see it work."

"You can't," said Zack. "It's not plugged in."

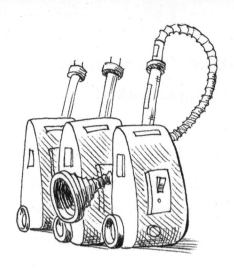

"No problem," squeaked Zingle. "I'll use my super Satpower."

She twiddled her antennae.

Ping!

Her Satpad flew out of her fur.

"Cosmic," said Tom.

"No, it is not cosmic," said Daisy. "Zingle, you mustn't zap *this* Hoover."

"OK, silly Earthling," squeaked Zingle. She aimed her Satpad at a nearby lawnmower. "I'll use it on that instead."

"No!" cried Daisy. "You mustn't use it on *anything* in the supermarket!"

It was too late.

Whizz! Bang! Crackle!

A sparkling beam of light shot out of the Satpad. The lawnmower roared into life, scattering the shoppers and cutting up the floor.

"Zoops!" squeaked Zingle. "That's interesting."

The supermarket manager appeared.

"I've heard all about you kids," he said sternly. "Charging about and making a mess of my store."

"That wasn't us," said Tom.

"It was our trolley," said Zack. "It's wonky."

"Your trolley couldn't have set off that lawnmower," insisted the manager.

"Oh, no," said Tom. "That was our . . ."

". . . mop," said Daisy, pointing at Zingle.

"I'm not a mop," squeaked Zingle.

"It's a talking mop," explained Tom.

"Talking mops don't set off lawnmowers," said the manager. "And, anyway, we don't sell talking mops. Pay for your shopping and leave at once!"

The friends grabbed two buns and a toothbrush for Zack's gran and paid at the checkout.

"We can't go home without Fizz!" said Daisy.

"I've got an idea," said Tom. "We'll go outside, put on false beards and come back inside in disguise to look for Fizz."

"Great idea," said Zack, "except we haven't got any false beards."

"Then I'll get some stilts and I'll put on a long coat and I'll pretend to be the owner of the supermarket and I'll make an announcement that all Earthlings have to go home – and that will just leave Fizz in here!" said Tom.

"You haven't got any stilts either," said Zack. "Or a long coat."

"Well, what are we going to do then?" asked Tom.

"I can see Fizz," squeaked Zingle suddenly. "On that moving thing."

Fizz was sitting on a conveyor belt, clutching a big box of Wheaty Krisps. He waved cheerfully at them.

"He's having a nice ride." Zingle's antennae wiggled with excitement. "Can I have a nice ride?"

"No," said Daisy.

"Someone's trying to buy him!" exclaimed Zack.

"They must think he's a toy," said Tom.

"We've got to rescue him," said Zack, "before he gets to the price scanner."

"You're right," said Tom. "It won't know how much a Satnik costs!"

"Quick, Zingle," said Daisy. "Use your super Satpower on that moving belt."

"Silly Earthling," squeaked Zingle, waving her Satpad. "You said I mustn't use it in the supermarket!"

"You can now," said Zack. "Make the belt go backwards."

Zingle aimed her Satpad at Fizz's conveyor belt.

Whizz! Bang! Crackle!

A sparkling beam of light hit the conveyor belt, but the conveyor belt didn't go backwards. It went forwards.

It whirred along at top speed, flinging all the shopping into the air.

"Zoops!" squeaked Zingle. "That's interesting."

The beam of light hit the other conveyor belts. They whirred along at top speed too.

Soon the air was full of flying shopping.

"Double zoops!" squeaked Zingle.
"That's even more interesting."

"But where's Fizz?" cried Zack.

Tom pointed over their heads. "There!"

Fizz was zooming over their heads,
along with a bunch of bananas, a box of
ice lollies and three packets of pasta. He
was still clutching his Wheaty Krisps.

"Catch him!" yelled Daisy.

They pushed and pulled the trolley
until it was underneath Fizz. Fizz and the
Wheaty Krisps landed with a bump next
to Zingle.

"That was exciting!" he said. "It was
even better than the time we got sucked
down that wormhole near Jupiter and all
our splitternocks flew off."

The beam of light hit the sprinklers in the ceiling. Everyone was showered with water.

"Silly Earthlings!" squeaked Zingle, sheltering under her new umbrella. "You said it doesn't rain in supermarkets."

The shoppers were rushing out of the supermarket. Tom, Zack and Daisy followed.

Zingle looked sad. "Shame we had to leave. I was having a lovely time."

"I'm glad I got my Wheaty Krisps," said Fizz happily.

"Wait a minute," said Zack. "We haven't paid for them!"

"We don't need to," said Fizz, showing them the empty box. "I ate them all before we came out."

"I'll go back in and pay when it stops raining in there," said Tom. "I'll say that one of the babies ate them."

"Can we come?" asked Fizz.

"Good idea," said Tom.

"No," said Zack. "It's a very bad idea."

"Are you sure?" asked Fizz.

"POSITIVE!" chorused Zack and Daisy.

"Never mind," squeaked Zingle. "We'll have a wonky trolley race when you get back."

"Cosmic!" said Tom.

NAME

Fizz

EARTH IDENTITY

satapoodle

REPORT

Young Earthlings are very strange. They think supermarkets are boring. They are wrong. Supermarkets are very exciting.

You can buy Wheaty Krisps.

NAME

Zingle

EARTH IDENTITY

blue mop-haired cat

REPORT

Earthlings don't like wonky trolleys. This is very strange, as wonky trolleys are much more interesting than ordinary trolleys. So are supermarkets. You can buy roofs. This is lucky, as it can rain in supermarkets.

Monkey Magic

Tom, Zack and Daisy were riding in the back of Tom's car. Tom's dad was taking them to Monkey Magic for the day.

"I've never been to Monkey Magic before," said Daisy. "I can't wait."

"It's cosmic," said Tom. "There are loads of high trees with ladders to climb . . ."

". . . and zip wires to zoom down . . ." said Zack.

". . . and monkeys to investigate!" squeaked Zingle.

Tom's dad had no idea that he was also taking four Satniks to Monkey Magic.

Fizz and Zingle were sitting in the boot with Toppo and Gronk.

Toppo lived in Tom, Zack and Daisy's classroom.

He pretended to be a zabbit – a cross between a zebra and a rabbit.

Gronk lived with Daisy.

He pretended to be a duck-billed parrotpuss. And since Daisy was an animal expert, everyone believed her when she said he was a rare kind of parrot.

Fizz's trumpet nose appeared over the back seat. "We know lots about

monkeys," he said. "A monkey grows
wool and goes *baa*."

"That's not a monkey," laughed Tom.
"That's a sheep."

"It's a monkey," said Fizz, wrinkling
his nose. "We looked them up."

Ping!

His Satpad flew out of his ear and
landed on his paw. He tapped the keys.

An image shimmered in the air.

"That's definitely a sheep," said Zack.

"That's a relief," said Toppo. "I don't think they'd be very good at climbing all those trees."

"I think the Satpad sprungles are still flobbered," said Gronk.

"Fizz was going to mend them yesterday," squeaked Zingle.

"Zoops!" said Fizz. "I forgot. I was too busy investigating the washing line."

"Then we'll have to find out about monkeys without the Satpads," said Toppo.

"But don't forget to stay hidden when we arrive at Monkey Magic," Daisy told the Satniks. "Pets aren't allowed."

"We don't need to hide," said Fizz. "We'll just pretend to be monkeys."

"When we've found out what monkeys do," added Toppo.

"There aren't any monkeys at Monkey Magic," said Zack.

"Silly Earthlings," squeaked Zingle. "I bet the place is full of monkeys."

"Why is it called Monkey Magic if there aren't any monkeys?" demanded Gronk.

"It's a place where Earthlings pretend to be monkeys," explained Tom. "Monkeys are good at climbing trees, you see."

"Here we are," called Tom's dad, stopping the car. "Everyone out."

"What fun!" squawked Gronk.

"Your voice has gone funny, Tom!" said his dad.

"It's the excitement," squawked Tom.

Dad gave him a funny look and marched off to buy the tickets.

Tom, Zack and Daisy jumped out of the car.

The Satniks jumped out after them. They looked up at the tall trees with their long rope ladders and high walkways and fast zip wires.

"This is much better than the climbing frame at school!" said Toppo, his ears curling up in excitement.

"It's even better than the Swishscrabbler Park back home!" exclaimed Fizz.

"And I can see some monkeys," said Gronk. "Up there in the trees."

"You were wrong, silly Earthlings," squeaked Zingle. "There *are* monkeys at Monkey Magic."

"I can't see any monkeys," said Daisy.

"Are they swinging about?" asked Tom eagerly.

"Not exactly," said Gronk.

"They're *fluttering* about," said Toppo.

"And going *coo, coo, coo*," squeaked Zingle.

"Cosmic!" said Tom. "I didn't know monkeys went *coo, coo, coo*. I thought they went *ooo, ooo, ooo*. Where are they?"

"There!" cried Fizz, pointing with his trumpet nose. "They must be really good at climbing trees – they've nearly got to the top!"

"They're not monkeys," said Zack. "They're pigeons."

"They haven't climbed the trees," explained Daisy. "They can fly."

"I knew that," said Gronk.

"This place should be called *Pigeon Magic*," said Toppo.

Dad came back with a man who had rope over his shoulder.

The Satniks scuttled out of sight under a bush.

"I'm Desmond and I'm your Monkey Monitor," the man told Tom, Zack and Daisy. "Good morning, monkeys!"

"Silly Earthling!" came a squeak from the bush. "There are no monkeys down here!"

The man looked at Tom. "That's true," he said. "But we *call* you all monkeys while you're here." He handed them some safety harnesses.

Then he read out a list of safety rules on a big board.

RULES

1. Always wear your safety harness.
2. Always clip yourselves onto the safety ropes.
3. Stay safe. No monkey madness.
4. Have lots of fun!

Tom, Zack and Daisy clipped on their safety harnesses and ropes. Desmond took Dad off to study a map of the route.

As soon as they were out of sight, Gronk poked his beak out of the bush.

"Those rules are no good for us!" he squawked indignantly.

"Don't worry," came Fizz's voice. "I've made a list of Satnik Safety Rules."

A list shimmered in front of the bushes.

Fizz's important list of Safety Rules
by Fizz
1. Children need safety harnesses.
2. Satniks don't need safety harnesses.
3. Have lots of fun.
4. Don't forget to look out for monkeys.

"That's a relief!" said Gronk. "Now we'll be safe too."

"Fizz is good at safety rules," squeaked Zingle.

"Come on, kids," called Tom's dad. "Follow me. I'll show you what to do."

He climbed a ladder that led up a very tall tree. Halfway to the top he got tangled in his harness.

"Help!" he cried as he fell off the ladder and dangled upside down from his rope.

Desmond rushed up.

"Grown-ups!" he sighed. "You three go on ahead while I get someone to sort him out."

Tom, Zack and Daisy climbed up to a platform in the trees.

They ran along a wobbly walkway high above the ground.

"Is anyone around?" asked Daisy.

"No," said Tom. "The coast is clear."

"You can come out now, Satniks," called Zack.

"Help!" came four Satnik voices from a nearby tree.

Toppo, Fizz, Zingle and Gronk were dangling upside down from a branch.

"Are you stuck?" asked Daisy anxiously.

"Of course not, silly Earthling," squeaked Zingle.

"Tom's dad showed us what to do," explained Fizz. "So we're doing it. I've put it on my safety list." He twisted his ear.

Ping!

His Satpad flew out and landed on his paw. A list shimmered upside down in the air.

"You don't want to take any notice of my dad," laughed Tom. "He's hopeless."

Fizz's new important list of safety rules by Fizz.
1. Children need safety harnesses.
2. Satniks don't need safety harnesses.
3. Have lots of fun.
4. Don't forget to look out for monkeys.
5. Dangle upside down.
6. Shout "Help!"

"Are you sure?" asked Toppo.

"Positive," said Tom. "Grown-ups are no good at Monkey Magic."

"Come and join us," said Zack. "We'll show you what to do."

"Good idea," said Toppo. "I'll use my super Satpower."

Ping!

Toppo's Satpad flew out of his ear and, in a flash, he'd waved it at his friends. The four little aliens floated slowly over to the walkway.

"What was that?" came a voice.

Desmond the Monkey Monitor was on the ground, looking up. The Satniks scurried into the leaves.

"Did you see some strange woodland creatures floating about?" Desmond called.

"No," said Daisy.

"That's true," whispered Tom. "The Satniks aren't woodland creatures."

"How odd," said Desmond. "I'm sure I saw something."

He walked away, scratching his head.

The Satniks popped out again.

"Last one to the next platform is a spliknummer!" yelled Toppo.

"What's that long shiny thing?" asked Gronk, as they all piled onto the platform.

"It's a washing line," said Fizz.

"I expect the monkeys hang their washing on it," squeaked Zingle.

"It's not a washing line," said Daisy. "It's a zip wire! We'll go first and you Satniks can follow."

"One at a time," added Zack.

"COSMIC!" yelled Tom as he zoomed to the ground after Zack and Daisy.

Fizz, Toppo and Zingle whizzed down in a bunch and knocked them all over.

There was a loud squawk and Gronk whizzed along the wire, somersaulted through the air and got his head wedged in a tree root.

"Are you OK, Gronk?" asked Daisy.

"I meant to do that," came Gronk's muffled voice. "I'm looking for monkeys in here."

"Have you found any?" asked Tom eagerly.

"As a matter of fact, I have," said Gronk. "There are lots. They're green and wriggly and they're very good at climbing trees."

"I knew we'd find them in the end," said Toppo happily.

Zack and Daisy pulled Gronk out and they all peered at the tree root.

"They're not monkeys," said Zack. "They're caterpillars."

"But soon they'll turn into—" began Daisy.

"Monkeys!" squeaked Zingle in delight.

"No," said Daisy. "Soon they'll turn into butterflies and moths."

"Not monkeys?" asked Gronk.

"Definitely not," said Zack.

"You Earthlings are strange," said Fizz. "This place should be called *Caterpillar Magic!*"

"Are you all right, monkeys?" came a shout.

The Satniks scooted up the nearest tree and hid.

Desmond the Monkey Monitor came crashing through the undergrowth.

"I'm sure those strange woodland creatures followed you down the zip wire," he said, looking anxiously around. "Did you see them? There was a stripy one, a peculiar-looking bird, a very small elephant . . . and a mop."

"I'm not a mop!" squeaked Zingle from the tree.

Desmond jumped in alarm. "Who said that?" he asked.

"It was me," said Tom in a squeaky voice. "I've not seen a mop — or anything strange."

"And that's true," he whispered to his friends. "The Satniks aren't strange. They're just ordinary aliens."

Desmond rubbed his eyes. "How odd," he said. "I must have been imagining things."

He set off down a path, peering
nervously into the bushes as he went.

Tom, Zack and Daisy climbed up to join
the Satniks.

Blublublub!

They all looked round to see where the
strange noise was coming from.

"Was that a monkey?" squeaked Zingle.

"Of course not!" squawked Gronk. "It was my tummy. I'm hungry."

"We've got lots of food in the car," said Tom. "We'll sit and eat it outside when we've finished all the climbing. That's called a picnic."

"Like those Earthlings are doing down there," said Fizz. A family were carrying a huge picnic basket along the path below. They spread a cloth on the ground, opened the basket and began to tuck in.

Gronk licked his beak with his long pink tongue. "Picnics look like a good thing to investigate," he said thoughtfully. "I'll just pop down and take a closer look."

Before anyone could stop him, Gronk leapt off the walkway. He tumbled through the air and landed upside down on a branch just above the picnickers.

"I meant to do that," he squawked, turning himself the right way up. His long tongue shot out, curled round a sandwich on a plate and slurped it back into his beak.

"Oh, no!" cried Daisy. "Gronk's going to be in big trouble!" She clipped her harness to a rope and swung down towards Gronk but, before she could grab him, Gronk took off, flapped away and bumped into a tree trunk.

"I meant to do that!" he squawked as he slid to the ground. "I'm off to investigate some more delicious picnics."

Daisy swung past and missed him again.

"Sausages!" squawked Gronk. He ran off towards a boy sitting on a bench. The boy had a sausage on a plate.

Slurrrrrp!

Gronk whipped it away with his tongue, swallowed it in one gulp and scampered away into a bush.

"Hey!" shouted the boy. "A bird just stole my sausage! MUM!"

He ran off.

"Got you!" exclaimed Daisy, as she swung past on her rope for the third time,

crashed through the bush, scooped up Gronk and swung back to the walkway.

"Cosmic rescue!" said Tom. "And just in time!"

The boy was back with his mum and Desmond the Monkey Monitor.

"Tell me exactly what the thief looked like," said Desmond.

"It was a peculiar-looking bird with a very long tongue," said the boy.

"I'll catch it," declared Desmond. "Where did it go?"

"Into that bush," said the boy.

Desmond dived into the bush.

The boy and his mum packed up their food and left.

"You mustn't take other people's food, Gronk," said Daisy. "And you nearly got caught."

"But I've just spotted a lovely big cake," said Gronk, flapping along the walkway. "There's enough for all of us."

"So there is," said Toppo, licking his lips.

Tom, Zack and Daisy peered down through the leaves. Another family had set out a picnic on a picnic table. In the middle was a huge cake covered in chocolate icing.

Desmond was marching up to the family

at the table. "There's a picnic-pinching bird on the loose," he told them. "I'm warning everyone to be careful." Then he rushed off.

The family hurriedly packed away their picnic.

"Zoops!" Gronk squawked in alarm. "My cake's leaving."

He flapped his wings, tripped over his feet and landed on his head in the middle of the table.

FUMP!

"I meant to do that," he told the astonished family.

His long tongue flew out towards the cake.

"It's the picnic-pinching bird!" yelped the boy.

"And it can talk!" exclaimed his sister.

"Catch it!" shouted their dad.

Tom, Zack and Daisy watched in horror as the children's mum picked Gronk up and dropped him into the picnic basket. She shut the lid and fastened the buckles.

"Let's find the Monkey Monitor," she said. "But we'll leave that thing here. It might be dangerous."

They rushed off.

"What a shame," squeaked Zingle. "That cake looked delicious."

"Never mind the cake!" exclaimed Zack. "We've got to rescue Gronk. Come on."

"But by the time we get down to the ground, those people will be back with Desmond," said Daisy.

"We could hold on to each other's feet and hang from the walkway," suggested Tom. "We might be able to reach him that way."

"That would take too long!" said Daisy.

Tom scratched his head. "We could get a great big piece of elastic, bungee-jump down, open the picnic basket, snatch Gronk and ping back up."

"Great idea," said Zack, "except we haven't got a great big piece of elastic."

"Well, there must be something we can do," said Tom.

"I know the very thing," announced Toppo. "It's time for a Top Toppo Trick."

"Cosmic!" said Tom. "That will cheer

us all up while we're working out how to rescue Gronk."

"This trick will cheer you all up *and* rescue Gronk at the same time," said Toppo. "Watch."

Ping!

His Satpad flew out of his ear. He waved it at the picnic basket. The basket rose slowly in the air until it came to rest on the walkway.

"Double cosmic!" exclaimed Tom, flinging open the lid. "You can come out now, Gronk."

"I would," mumbled Gronk, his beak full of sandwich, "but the kind family left some food in here for me. It would be rude not to finish it up."

"We'll help!" shouted Fizz, Toppo and Zingle, jumping in next to him.

"No!" cried Tom, Zack and Daisy.

They were too late. The Satniks had eaten every scrap.

At that moment, Desmond the Monkey Monitor came tiptoeing up to the table below. He was carrying a net and a large cage.

He looked around the table.

He looked under the table.

He looked under the tablecloth.

"No picnic-pinching bird in a picnic basket here," he muttered crossly. "Where has it gone?"

"Looks like Desmond needs cheering up," whispered Toppo from the basket. "Time for another Top Toppo Trick."

"Good idea!" Tom whispered back.

"It is *not* a good idea!" hissed Daisy.

But it was too late.

The Satniks hopped out of the picnic basket.

Toppo waved his Satpad over it.

The basket rose from the walkway, floated gently downwards and hovered right in front of Desmond.

Desmond froze as the basket circled slowly round him.

"It doesn't seem to be cheering him up," said Fizz.

"That's strange," said Toppo, scratching his head. "It's one of my best Top Toppo Tricks."

"I'll try," said Gronk. "I'll get my Satpad to make the soothing sound of the knock-kneed satcrow."

Ping!

His Satpad flew into his outstretched claw and he tapped the keys with his beak.

A dreadful screeching noise filled the air.

Desmond gave a yelp and staggered off with his hands over his ears.

"That was a lovely picnic," said Fizz, rubbing his round tummy.

"Deliciously scrumptious," agreed Toppo.

"Now, let's get exploring," said Gronk.

"This way," said Tom, pointing along the walkway.

Zingle scampered ahead.

"What's that?" she squealed, pointing a paw at a large cardboard shape nailed to a tree.

"That's a monkey," said Zack.

"No, it's not," said Fizz. "It's flat. Earth animals aren't flat."

"And it's not going *ooo, ooo, ooo*," said Gronk.

"And it doesn't look very good at climbing," said Toppo.

"That's because it isn't a *real* monkey," explained Daisy. "It's just a cardboard cut-out."

The Satniks looked disappointed.

"Never mind," said Tom. "We're the monkeys today! And we've got lots more fun climbing to do."

"Uh-oh!" said Zack. "Here comes Desmond."

"With his net and his cage!" added Daisy.

"Don't worry," said Toppo. "Time for another Top Toppo Trick! Desmond will definitely like this one."

He waved his Satpad into the trees. The ropes, the nets, the swings and the walkways all rose in the air and tangled themselves into the most amazing shapes.

Desmond dropped his net and his cage and ran off, gibbering with fright.

"Great trick, Toppo!" laughed Zack. "Monkey Magic is better than ever!"

"I'm calling it Monkey Madness now!" Toppo said.

They all climbed the long twisting
ladder that wound up to the top of
the trees.

"Wait for me!" came a shout.

Tom's dad was climbing up towards them.

"Help!" he yelled as he slipped and
dangled upside down.

"We'd better rescue him," said Daisy.

"OK," said Tom, "after we've explored
Toppo's new Monkey Madness."

They ran along the walkways.

They swung on the
long ropes.

They dived into the
bouncy nets.

They jumped onto the last zip wire. It
twisted through the trees at top speed.

"This is better than the best rollercoaster
in the world!" exclaimed Zack.

"In the universe!" squeaked Zingle.

"It's totally COSMIC!" yelled Tom.

REPORT

NAME

Toppo

EARTH IDENTITY

zabbit

REPORT

Big Earthlings and little Earthlings love climbing about in trees at something called Monkey Magic. This is a strange name as the monkeys are flat and can't climb. Grown-up Earthlings are not very good at climbing.

Monkey Magic was a bit too easy. I think I've fixed that.

ADDITION TO TOPPO'S REPORT

NAME

Gronk

EARTH IDENTITY

duck-billed
parrotpuss

REPORT

Earthling picnics are very tasty but they are
not very easy to find. A bit like monkeys.

the

orion star

★ ★ ★